Swimming!

Lauren Tobia

They're so

tumbly,

wiggly,

jumbly!

Can YOU
do it, too?

ISBN 978-1-4063-6185-8 ◆ www.walker.co.uk ◆ 10 9 8 7 6 5 4 3 2 1

Peep through the steamy windows,
Pu-u-u-ush the heavy door.
"We're going swimming!"
shout Billy and Bee.
**"Take care on the
puddly floor!"**

ISLINGTON

Please return this item on or before the last date stamped below or you may be liable to overdue charges. To renew an item call the number below, or access the online catalogue at www.islington.gov.uk/libraries. You will need your library membership number and PIN number.

07/19

1 8 MAR 2018

1 2 AUG 2019

2 0 SEP 2023

1 2 FEB 2020

1 8 MAY 2024

0 8 APR 2022

1 9 AUG 2024

1 3 JUN 2022

Islington Libraries

Let's Go

Caryl Hart

Bee and Billy,

Billy and Bee,

See what they

can do!

WALKER BOOKS

AND SUBSIDIARIES

LONDON · BOSTON · SYDNEY · AUCKLAND

For Mum, who gave me a love of water ≈ C.H. ▾▲▾ To Kate and Georgia Holyfield ≈ L.T.
First published 2019 by Walker Books Ltd, 87 Vauxhall Walk, London SE11 5HJ ◆ Text © 2019 Caryl Hart
Illustrations © 2019 Lauren Tobia ◆ The right of Caryl Hart and Lauren Tobia to be identified as author and illustrator
respectively of this work has been asserted by them in accordance with the Copyright, Designs and Patents Act 1988

Bee pulls her shoes and socks off,

Billy builds a heap of clothes.

They wriggle into swimsuits...

Ready?

Steady?

GO!

Funny Bee loves splashing,

SPLOSH! She jumps straight in.

Doggy paddle – kick-kick-kick,

"Billy! Watch me swim!"

Billy dip-dip-dabbles toes,

Then down the steps with Mummy.

He slides into the glassy pool,

Water chilly on his tummy.

"I'm a pirate, ARRR!"
shouts Bee.

"Climb aboard
my ship!"

But Billy holds on tight to Mummy,
He's worried he might slip.

Together, they search
for sharks and crabs,
Bee crawls across
the float.

Then wibble-wobbles-tumbles ...

SPLASH! She's fallen off their boat!

Here's Mummy to the rescue,

With little Baby Boo.

Bee coughs and splutters,

   blinks and laughs!

Then Billy

   jumps in, too!

They kick and glide, splish and splosh,
Then Billy needs
a wee!

Climb out and find the bathroom,

"Quick, quick!

Follow me!"

Now Billy, Bee
and Baby Boo,
Are floating on
their backs.

Three giggly squiggly starfish,

"Well done!" Mummy claps.

But Baby starts to sniffle,

It's time to clamber out.

Bee clings on to the railings,

"Not yet! Not yet!" she shouts.

Then Billy does a shower dance,

He's covered in shampoo.

"My name is Mr Bubble Head!"

Bee feels better.

"Do me, too!"

Billy wriggles his wrinkly fingers,
Bee dries her crinkly toes.
Three snuggly-buggly bundles,

Pulling on warm, dry clothes.

Sniffs and drips
    and crunchy crisps,
Baby Boo's asleep.
Billy and Bee
    are happy-floppy,
They'll swim again
    next week.

Bee and Billy
are going home,
Today has been
such fun.
They're yawny,
sleepy, snuggly,
tired...

**Goodbye,
everyone!**